IF I WERE

IF I WERE

DIVYA PRAKASH

A BOOK BY DP72

Enter Caption

About the Author

The name of the author of this story is Divya Prakash aka DP72 who is 18 years old, and he hails from Patna. His father's name is Dinesh Kumar and mother's name is Madhuri Lata, apart from this, he also has a sister whose name is Divya Jyoti. His works include Saniya, Govinda Gopalam, Sakhi etc.

Enter Caption

Summary

It is the story of a brother and sister, in which a brother tells his sister a fictional story of a couple named Harry and Sia.

Enter Caption

IF I WERE

My name is Rohit, and I am 20 years old, and I am writer I used to write stories from childhood but never dreamed of becoming

Enter Caption

a writer but once there was no electricity in my house for two days.

I was alone at home with my sister, then my sister told me that I am getting bored, there is no electricity in the house for two

Enter Caption

a writer but once there was no electricity in my house for two days.

I was alone at home with my sister, then my sister told me that I am getting bored, there is no electricity in the house for two

Enter Caption

days, I have not even watched TV for two days, you write stories, So, can you please tell me a story of yours?

I was amazed because my sister once showed interest in listening to

Enter Caption

any of my stories, but at that point she said there shouldn't be a much bigger story. This was a matter of concern for me because I did not write many short stories and at that time, I did not even

Enter Caption

have any short stories ready.

My sister was hoping that I would tell her a good story, so I didn't want to break her hopes.

Enter Caption

Harry, in which Harry is a lazy man and doesn't want to do any kind of work and puts all the blame on Sia whenever he makes a mistake.

Enter Caption

After this I started the story and said Harry and Sia are two couple who got married recently and now they live in their flat.one day Sia was cutting her nails and Harry was sitting under the closed fan and watching TV.

Enter Caption

At the same time, Harry turns into a strange face and shouts in a loud voice, hey, why is this fan is off, man.

Enter Caption

Sia replied if there is such a problem then turn on the fan yourself.

Harry responds yes, it's you, so you are telling me to turn on the fan, if I were I would never do it because I don't

Enter Caption

impose my work on others like you.

Sia replied, you are useless, Sia goes and turn on the fan. The trash on the fan goes to Harry's eyes after which Harry closes his eyes and angrily says

Enter Caption

to Sia, why do you forget to clean the fan, if I were I would always clean the fan.

Sia reminds Harry, look at the calendar, this week you had to clean the fan and you forgot. Harry says it's

Enter Caption

corner, because of which I forgot to clean the fan, if I were I would put the calendar in front, so that people keep looking at the calendar time to time but don't worry, bring me the broom I just clean the fan.

Enter Caption

After that Sia was standing and she was holding the table and harry was standing on the table and cleaning the fan, meanwhile the broom slipped from his hand and goes straight on Sia's

Enter Caption

head, because of that Sia's balance gets disturbed, and she falls to the ground, and she also misses the table from her hand, then Harry also loses his balance and falls.

Enter Caption

My sister was now showing interest in my story.

So, I went ahead with the story, and I said:

Sia was rubbing her hurt head and Harry was rubbing his back on the other side, which was hurt due to

Enter Caption

were, I would hold the table properly and not let it fall

Now Sia was very angry, and she went to another room. Finally, when Sia was locked herself in the room, Harry said that

Enter Caption

this is you, who was locked herself in the room due to the mistake of yourself, I would have left the house, if I were.

Hearing my story my sister laughed out loud, she was my

Enter Caption

sister whose laugh made me dream of becoming a writer, I would never have been a writer if I were.

Enter Caption

Enter Caption

Contents

9 798886 842456

Printed by Libri Plureos GmbH in Hamburg,
Germany